fatal obsession

surviving an extramarital

Zsofia

Outskirts Press, Inc.
Denver, Colorado

This is a work of fiction. The events and characters described herein are imaginary and are not intended to refer to specific places or living persons. The opinions expressed in this manuscript are solely the opinions of the author and do not represent the opinions or thoughts of the publisher. The author has represented and warranted full ownership and/or legal right to publish all the materials in this book.

Fatal Obsession
Surviving An Extramarital
All Rights Reserved.
Copyright © 2009 Zsofia
v2.0

This book may not be reproduced, transmitted, or stored in whole or in part by any means, including graphic, electronic, or mechanical without the express written consent of the publisher except in the case of brief quotations embodied in critical articles and reviews.

Outskirts Press, Inc.
http://www.outskirtspress.com

ISBN: 978-1-4327-4711-4

Outskirts Press and the "OP" logo are trademarks belonging to Outskirts Press, Inc.

PRINTED IN THE UNITED STATES OF AMERICA

In the loving memory of my parents

Preface

Extramarital affairs happen in our society when one partner goes outside of the marriage due to emotional or physical needs. Often such affairs blow apart and meet a dead end in their infancy. There are lots of marriage counselors and divorce lawyers who support and counsel the hurt party, the husband or the wife who becomes the victim of cheating by their partner. But nobody discusses about and supports the one who cheats, especially the woman who genuinely gets emotionally involved. Nobody even talks about her abyss, and the society around us treats the affair only as a pursuit to physical satisfaction. This is the story of a woman who gets into such an extramarital affair, and is left to live with the love and immense sadness in her heart. I thought of sharing this with the world, and especially with the victimized wives, who never try to look into the other side of the story, and with those typical husbands who are weak-minded when they start an affair and remains the same till the end of it. The world doesn't end for anybody; nobody stops living their life, but people are changed forever due to such incidents.

I am thankful to the one who shared her deep, painful experiences with me and helped me weave her pain into a novel for others to read. Writing this word by word and day by day was like living those moments again. I cannot change her life, her past, but I can try to let others look at the other side of the coin.

I am thankful to my family, for cooperation and moral support while I was burning the midnight oil to finish this, and to my little son who showed patience after understanding what I was trying to do.

Special thanks to Manmath Rajput and a young designer, Anupriya Rajput, for their contributions in designing the cover for the book and supporting me in my need.

I would also like to thank Larry Morando, who guided me and was always there while the book went into production.

Fatal Obsession
Surviving an extramarital

A cool breeze was all around me on the dark terrace, and I was gazing at the stars, feeling very lonely at heart. Thinking about why I felt so depressed and mournful, I was deliberating – Is there something missing from my life? Why I was feeling dead, with no energy to cope mentally with anything? After many sessions with myself, alone on the dark terrace, I realized that I NEED LOVE and that was something missing from my life. I was craving an adoring hug and was thirsty for affectionate touch. I was realizing how much I was in need of all this.

This revelation instantly made me anxious that I should be in love with somebody. Now the question was: how to find love? Where to find it? Love was missing from my life because my husband was industrious in his career and was constantly struggling with his aspirations to earn a salary comparable to what a proficient IT professional such as I could earn. Somehow just after six months of our marriage the downfall of his career started. He was losing sleep, his mind, and eventually his relationship with me to maintain his self-esteem and male ego. He changed the definition of love per his convenience -- to make an effort to earn for the family, and to be mechanically physical with his wife on the bed, meant love. This definition could not be the basis of a relationship to connect two hearts together. For me, sex and making love are two different things. Hence my heart could not accept his definition and parameters for love, and I was growing further away from him day by day, month by month, and year by year until seven long years passed and I understood that Love was the missing integral element of my life, and I should pursue it vigorously.

Lovely Ladies, reading this, understand that tension in the marriage can happen when the wife brings more moolah home than her husband does. The husband; consciously and subconsciously, gets into a sort of competition with you that goes on and on for years. Horizons are widened forever, married couples are separated, but the competition seems never ending. When you know that this is happening, initially you try hard to overcome this antagonism, but over a period of time, you start losing patience, emotionally and mentally. His struggle becomes your pain and the reason for your loneliness. If this is happening with you and your married life is not giving you the warmth you need to survive, due to whatever reason, and all your endeavors to fix it are ineffectual, then beware of the fact that you might start looking for somebody whose company can actually give you some pleasure and allow you to feel your feminine virtues. Putting it bluntly, your chances of falling in love and getting into an extramarital affair are high.

All gentlemen, if you are into the marathon for more earnings, please stop and realize that she loves you and she needs you more than your money; she wants to be in your arms, wants to whisper love in your ears, and you are the center of her life -- she respects you without your monetary power. She admires the way you won her heart, caressed her often and melted her on the bed every time. Money is really secondary in life and it doesn't matter whether it's coming through her or you, the pool remains the same. Please don't waste the golden period of your romance and love. Isn't it shattering to snatch yourself away from her when she needs you most, and loves you more than anything in this world? You need to understand this. Once you fail, may not get another chance.

Back to my loneliness -- the desire to fall in love was burning inside me and my subconscious was ready to find it, though I was wondering what might change in my life to let this happen. I was an introverted, solitude-loving person who never took the first step to start a conversation until I was already on friendly terms with people, and I had only one close friend, whom I had known since childhood.

Miraculously, next day in the office I came to know that I got an assignment in the US for three months, and I would have to leave India shortly. I did not receive any cosmic signal that today would be the day when my life and I myself as a person would change forever.

ZSOFIA

I was busy in the office making arrangements, procuring the mandatory paperwork, and taking care of all those eleventh hour preparations when I was called to a meeting for that new assignment, on which a team of twenty was already working. I was exhausted to my limits, got shoe bites and was barely able to stand. Reluctantly I entered the small meeting room, where I did not get a chair to sit. My manager, a cool personality, married, father of two young boys, with whom I had working for the past year and a half, called this meeting at the end of the day to scold few people and make others learn a lesson. Everybody was listening quietly when he started with the laundry list of reprimands. He was making eye contact with everyone except me, as I was the newest one on this project. He was lecturing about this and that and went on and on for an hour and a half. I was constantly staring at him and was wondering – When he will stop? Then suddenly I got an exhilarating thought in my mind that if he didn't stop in the next minute, I would close his lips with mine to stop him saying another word. For few seconds I was fantasizing a gentle kiss and feeling the heat of his breath and then I realized, Oh My God! What the heck I am thinking? Something started in my mind, my sensations were lost, and suddenly I felt he was a totally different person in front of me. Mentally I felt so close to him. For women, all physical relations are mental first. After I imagined it, my eyes were focused on the floor instead of his face; I was blushing, smiling, and hoping that nobody was looking at me. After few minutes the meeting ended, and I figured out that I was mentally absent. Without facing him I quickly came out of the room. While driving way back home, his face and that kiss kept flashing in my mind. And the very next day I left for the US.

Now that I was in the US, my new assignment was keeping me busy during the day, and thoughts about my manager were boggling my mind at night. I was alone in the US, without family or loved ones, in a hotel room. I was striving to keep thoughts of him away from my mind, as I knew it would be dangerous for my job and in future -- how uneasy it would be for me to work normally and professionally with him.

This was the beginning of my "Fatal Obsession," and this is how we define "Obsession": A thought that persistently recurs despite your attempts to resist it. An obsession provokes anxiety and dominates a person, although the person regards it as being senseless.

That's exactly what happened with me. I couldn't resist fantasizing about him till my eyes closed at night and slowly, the fantasies unleashed my wildness. Someone has written that sensual pleasures have the fleeting brilliance of a comet. I started glowing from inside due to that brilliance. Days and nights were spent with thoughts of him, and after a month, I came to the conclusion; that I should tell him about how I felt for him. My heart was skipping beats while I was thinking about telling him. I had no idea how to express my feelings. Day by day it was becoming harder for me to carry the burden of those hidden feelings for him. Every time when I reported to him about the new assignment, my heart started racing and my voice would shake. I tried to evaluate all the pros and cons of my professional and personal life, but somehow couldn't control what was going on in my mind.

I was trying to think harder how to start and create a scenario to tell him. One day I asked him whether he had any official plans to come to the US. He simply said no. Then another day over the weekend when I saw him online on instant messenger, I just couldn't control myself and thought it should be now or never. I started the confession of my feelings with the simple sentence, "I like you," and then after a while he responded, "OK." Then I wrote, "I like you, and I mean it differently." Chatting went on for more than two hours, and I was successfully able to convey the message, about how I felt for him. After doing that, I was scared, as my consciousness was constantly hammering my mind not to do it -- I might be in danger of losing my job. But I just could not control myself. I was not able to believe that I'd done it. He explained to me that his life was also missing something which he was not able to define clearly, and he was always busy in continuing with what he had. In next few days, chatting and phone conversations reached to the level of discovering each other's hidden treasures. Meticulously we shared our likes, dislikes, hobbies, and interests, and often asked each other intimate questions in order to understand each other's favorite pursuits.

I started missing him badly -- my nights were restless, I wanted to kiss him, feel him, and wanted to make love to him. His condition was somewhat similar; he was feeling excited about everything that was going on. Being a good manager, he might have never thought about me the way he was thinking now. Those feelings were bit scary for him, considering his position in the organization and his professional relationship with me. But somehow he was also not able to control what was going on, and just kept going with the flow. He too was now deep into it, although he had never imagined allowing something like this to happen. Being an emotional man, he always showered his loved ones with his care and love. He was considerate with me in his approach, and his wildness was unleashed too in telling me about his fantasies and hidden desires. People like him appear to be very strong and emotionally balanced but are very sensitive inside, and most of the time refrain from indulging in emotional entanglements, as it's hard for them to handle the pain afterward, but when it happens, it happens and just cannot be stopped.

We were destined to meet -- finally that day came, and due to some urgent business he was also scheduled to travel to the US at the same place and the same hotel where I was. Both of us were pretty excited to meet each other, but were afraid and hesitant about our first reactions, as we had never met each other on these terms, and things were no longer just professional between us. Distances were diminished and so was the line holding us apart.

I was waiting outside my hotel room as he called me up and said he had landed and would shortly arrive at the hotel.

And then came the breathtaking moment when he was in front of me, this time as a new person whom I had known on an intimate level for just two months -- he was not the one with whom I had been working for the past year and a half. I somehow was not able to look into his eyes, and after a brief Hi & Hello he came into the room. Now he was in front of me as a different person. My mind was debating whether to accept his personality as an individual other than the one to whom I reported as a Manager. I was nervous and it was visible from my actions, the way I was restlessly walking around the room and trying hard to be normal. He gauged my nervousness and after few minutes of talking about his long journey, he asked me to sit down near him so that he could relax and hold my hands. I obeyed like I was numb, and hesitantly hugged him -- before I uttered a word, his lips closed mine, only to remind me, that was what I had visualized at first. The warmth of his touch invaded the shell that had encapsulated him and me together during the last two months. For a long time we were lip-locked, and then slowly he rubbed his cheek against mine, and planted kiss after the kiss on my neck, slowly moving down to listen to my heart beating in ecstasy. I closed my eyes. Delicately his hands were exploring my dimensions and challenging all my senses. Being bashful, I kept shrinking until he made a bold move. An hour later I found myself bare on the bed, with only sheets on me. We made love several times and I felt like the bird inside me got wings today and she could fly high. I felt so light and full of life suddenly, it appeared to me that this is what I had been searching for, and this is what I needed. He made me feel like a woman again, and gave me the sense of completeness which was totally missing from my life. His lovemaking was intoxicating, and the way he caressed me artistically and lovingly was undoubtedly something that I'd never had before. We were cuddling and fondling each other, and after dinner, he got up to go to his room to sleep for the rest of the night. I was not very comfortable about the fact that he did not want to stay with me, after we had made love and had been so close for a month, although right from the beginning he was trying to define the rules for our adventurous relationship and specified few times that we would not give any emotional baggage to each other and let this relationship be purely for fun. I agreed every time, ignorant of my true feelings. I did not put my mind to actually decoding what he meant, as I never had any such relationship in my life.

Here comes the debate in my mind that I was actually in "Need" of him, that I didn't just "Want" him. And he just wanted me he didn't need me. So right from the beginning the Rules of the Game were different for each of us. He wanted me to fulfill his desire, which in turn was my way to satisfy my need to be loved. Before approaching men, a woman should always be very clear and confident about whether she needs a man, or just wants a man. That's what decides the fate of the relationship. And the guys are smart enough to behave per the woman's perspective. If she is too much into trying for a long term relationship, they can make any number of false promises, which they already know they are not going to fulfill. While if the man realizes right from the beginning that the woman is seeking a man only for a short term adventure, then he takes it easy and do not indulge in too many lies. So please clarify in your mind what you want, and then go for it. The chemistry of an extramarital affair is different from the other relationships in life, and it should be handled differently, but only if you know how to do it. And like many others, I didn't know how I should handle it.

When I saw him getting ready to leave the room, I tried hard not to say a word, but eventually expressed myself that he could – well actually, he *should* -- sleep with me. After I insisted, he stayed with me in my room and we slept together --, I do not remember how many times I hugged him and kissed him in between sleeping. I was feeling secure, calm, and relaxed in his arms, the way I never felt before. I was peacefully restless the whole night, and was wondering that I knew him since last so many lives and he does not appear somebody new, entered into my world. I kept thinking about whether it was right or wrong -- which direction was I moving in, and what would happen tomorrow?

The next day, our daily office routine started, and life continued with him. Everything was different right from the first moment in the morning -- going to office together, kissing him in the car park, expecting to get a glimpse of him while working, watching him out of the corner of my eyes, smiling for no reason, behaving boldly and professionally for work and then coming back from the office craving a hug, sometimes cooking for him, all was embedded into my daily routine. Our evening hugs always turned into naughty, lovely intimate encounters, at times fulfilling each other's fantasies, and finally resulting into sleeping and holding each other close. I was living with him as a separate body but one soul. I slowly started realizing that this was love, real love, but was scared to tell him due to his rule – that we would not be an emotional burden to each other while we were involved. I had fear in my mind that he would become detached, if I told him, so I was hiding it deeply, feeling pain and pleasure both in doing so.

One day he did not come back with me from the office, as he had to go with his friend, and I was not aware of where he would be. I was alone in the room waiting for hours, when suddenly a strange thought popped up in my mind that *He might have gone to the pub to see those girls out there.* We had shared our fantasies, so my mind said he must be realizing them. This thought made me angry and insecure, and I made a judgment in my mind that he should not do that. It was like a breach of trust in love. But wait!!! Who was in love? While waiting and thinking about his fantasy, I started drinking --, I was jealous, full of anguish. I drank a few bottles of beer and then went outside in the freezing cold and kept standing and waiting there. The cold was penetrating my bones and was unbearable. I did not understand until now -- why was I punishing myself? Yes!! It was a punishment for indulging in one sided love that started far too early.

At last when he came back, he asked me why did I drink that much? I cried and confessed that I loved him, just loved him too much and didn't know when it started, and I could not stand his fantasies and could not share him with anybody else except his wife. He got the shock of his life, as he wasn't expecting anything like that, at least so early. He appeared overwhelmed and confused about his feelings for me. I never came to know whether he had any similar feelings for me or not, at that time. But somehow I feel that neither was that a foul play for him, nor he can truly classify it as love. Maybe that was what I wanted to believe? Something inside him was holding him back from admitting his true feelings -- something which I was not able to imagine. He was still in that initial analysis phase of the cataclysmic events that were changing his life too. Without reacting to my confession of love, he told me where he was, and assured me that there was no need to be suspicious about anything. He held me in his arms, kissed me softly and passionately, and I melted. I don't remember for how long I kept loving and kissing him. That day I truly understood that while you are drunk, you lose control over your body, but your mind still works perfectly.

Love just sparked inside me and I couldn't even realize, how swiftly it made a place inside my heart. It was a signal of a problem coming down the road, and I should have recognized it that time. I should have realized that the sky was going to fall on my head one day, but I was lost, lost, and lost in that pure and divine feeling of love. Extramarital affairs become torment when you fall in love with the one who has a predetermined set of rules so as not to indulge emotionally. Infinite care should be taken until both partners are sure to share the same feelings. Never sail one sided -- you will be drowned, and only you will be the one suffering in the end. It is better to be controlled and safe than sorry -- which I wasn't.

The next morning, I was worried about my previous night's confession to him and was silently trying to understand his actions and reactions. Though scared of the detachment, I knew that I had lost control over my heart and my mind, and all this happens when we are in love. I felt pain deep inside, deciding that he didn't get it. It started raining and I stood at the door to feel it -- I intentionally asked him to search for a song for me on the internet by "F.R. David" with the lyrics: "Words don't come easy, to me, how can I find a way, to make you see, I love you, Words don't come easy." He played the song and was smiling at me, as if to ask, "Why?" I looked at him to try to decipher what he was thinking. But our relationship was too new for us to read each other well, and his expressions were very limited. After day or two I gave up, thinking that I loved him and that was my truth, and I might as well let things take their own course while going forward. I was open in front of him now, and often while hugging and loving him I used to say "I love you," and he used to respond with a smile, saying "OK."

One day a group of friends from my office invited me to a late night party at a pub which was twenty-eight miles away. Initially I said "No" to them, as I did not want to annoy my love by leaving him alone, but then they pressured me too much, and I had to agree. I called my love to tell him that I would be leaving that night to respond to an invitation, and would be back late. He sounded "OK" over the phone, and told me that he would also be late, as he was having dinner at his friend's house. I dressed up, mulling over the dilemma of whether it would really be OK with him or not. When one of the guys from my group came to pick me up, I thought, so what if I am going without my love? After all, he is also enjoying dinner at his friend's house -- then why should I be worried? While on the way, I was chit-chatting with the guy, and in the back of my mind remembering and missing my love, when finally we reached that noisy pub and met the rest of the group. The guy with me, whom I had met only a month ago, suddenly appeared to be very caring. He was holding me around the waist while we were looking for our group, and gently pushing the other guys aside to help me make my way as I walked inside. I considered it a safeguard, as at times it's risky to be alone in such places. After reaching the group, I started talking to one of my female friends while drinking, and then I danced for few minutes; then she left the dance floor, leaving me alone with the guy who had picked me up. We were drinking, and he started dancing with me, and slowly I realized that his dance moves were becoming sensual, and he was getting closer and closer to me. The next minute, before I could do anything, he sort of grabbed me so that I had to push him away, and the drink I was holding dropped to the floor and made my socks wet and sticky. He got it and didn't make any other advances till he dropped me back at the hotel. I was silent and upset on the way back as I came to realize what my friends had in mind for me, and how I was unaware of the fact that the "One" who came to pick me up liked me, and it was sort of a date setting.

I came back and entered into the room silently and found that my love had not slept yet. It was 2:30 AM and I was not expecting him to be awake that late, as usually he went to sleep on time. Though I was upset, I figured out that he was restless and uselessly walking in the room. While changing, I told him that one of my socks got wet and he sarcastically said, "I don't know what people do, so that their socks get wet." I smiled back, as I was surprised at what I'd just heard. That was a jealous statement inspired by love, and seeing that in his eyes, I hugged him tightly and assured him that I loved him too much and would never go out again like this. That night while loving and sleeping together, whenever I said, "I love you," he responded with "Me too." I was very happy, on one hand, and was feeling guilty about leaving him alone, on the other hand. I could not explain to him what had happened in the pub, and how my evening had gone. I had no desire to give him more pain. Lots of confusing thoughts clouded my mind, things difficult to sort out -- was that love, was he really in love with me, the way I was with him? Or was it simply his manly desire to control me on personal grounds too, considering that professionally already he was in command and authority? Despite of the conflicting possibilities, I was enjoying the mere thought of his falling in love with me.

Over the weekend, some of our colleagues planned a trip

to Atlantic City and New York which included few hours' drive one way, and an overnight stay. We two were together, surrounded by five others. We were finding it hard just to hold each other's hands, and to even look at each other. At times my actions were daring and naughty and he was trying his level best to control me. I was always out of my mind and out of this world whenever he was with me. I even dared to kiss him on the cold Atlantic Beach where I don't know who from the group of our colleagues, might have been looking at us, or from where. Our love affair should be kept secret, due to our married status and professional relationship. I still get chills when I think about what I did and where I did it. I intentionally used to walk slowly, so we were left behind and I could hold his hand, and he used to try to pull it back with all his strength. He was horrified by my daring attempts, but I was busy all the time playing my lovely, naughty pranks on him. After we came back from the trip, till today whenever I look at those snaps, I always wonder – Oh! So this is what the Atlantic beach and the boardwalk looked like. I wasn't at that place, I was only with him.

We lived together for nine days and at last the day came when he had to leave for India. I asked him to stay for few more days, but he was unable to. I was trying to explain to myself that it would be all right, but started feeling the pain of living without him at the same place, being lonely inside that same room, restlessly curling up on the same bed without holding him next to me, squeezing the pillow in my arms instead of him. It was horrifying for me. Finally, the moment he left, I felt like all my energy, my blood had been drained out of my body -- I kept standing outside for a long time, senseless, trying hard to control myself. It felt like the world was going far away from me, mile by mile, and I wasn't able to handle the wreckage -- I cried loudly after going inside the room. His departure was devastating for me; I cried and shivered until he called from the airport, and while talking to him I was wishing and praying that he would come back, just once, and I would hold him so tightly and would never let him go far away or get separated from me. I remember the way he was looking at me while leaving; he was feeling helpless and trying to realize the pain in my eyes.

And after he boarded the plane, I realized where I was and what had just happened with me in the last nine days, how I had transformed into a totally different person; I felt like I didn't know myself and that my life had just taken a U- turn; I had no control over myself, and I remember that it felt like a strange sensation. I had a feeling that night that his love and he as a person now lived with me inside my heart, my mind, my body, and my soul. The more I tried not to think about him, the more I missed my breaths. I was feeling his touch even though he wasn't there, I was talking to him in my mind even though he was not there to listen, I was holding him close to me, I was resting my head on his bare chest and I was kissing him all the time. These feelings were so deep inside me that I was even day-dreaming of his presence all around me, in whatever I did, no matter, wherever I am. This was the deadly thing that started happening to me which I didn't know how to handle or properly identify.

Every day, I didn't even have the courage to go inside my room again and deal with that loneliness, but I had to; there was no choice, I had to work a month longer for my US assignment. In the office, inside the elevators, near to my seat, inside my car he was omnipresent, even though he was gone. It was very difficult for me to stay in the office, to come back to that hotel room again. Slowly I was losing my conscious senses and my interest in everything and was in the process of learning to live with his memory.

After he reached India, our romance continued over the phone and chat sessions, and we were waiting for each other desperately. We were also thinking about how we would be handling all this in India where family and acquaintances would be close all around. We knew that it was going to be very difficult for us to find a time and place where we could be one body and one soul again secretively.

And the day came when finally I got back to India with my family again. My husband appeared to me like a stranger, and that was quite obvious, because mentally I hadn't been with him for so long, and physically I had been away from him for the past three months. I tried hard to behave normally, but something inside me was changed; I was finding it very difficult to be in bed with him, and was looking for all sorts of reasons not to indulge that normal behavior of married life. Every time it felt like nothing more than a forced act of trying to cooperate, and it broke a woman inside me for hours and days. I was not feeling the intensity of him or his love. I had gone far, far away from him and it was visible from the way I started dressing up for the office, all the time singing, smiling for no reason. I was lost in my new world of happiness. At times I was even teasing my husband by saying, What if I found somebody other than you? But he used to make fun of me, as he was habitually taking me for granted.

Now back in our India office, we two were trying to behave normally and to find hidden moments to tease each other or say something. He used to sit inside a Glass Cabin and he assigned me a cubicle from which I could see him and he could see me. Though we needed to be very careful, quite a few times I had to go to his Glass Cabin to discuss work, and that was the time when I used to release my breath which I'd been holding since first thing in the morning, just to talk to him once and say something lovely or naughty. At times other Managers also entered the room at the same time, to talk to him, and I used to chew my lips in helpless annoyance. There were incidents when both of us had to have a meeting with few other people and I used to kiss him with my eyes and I used to pout my lips while in meetings to tease him, and for him it was really hard not to smile at that. He always smiled even after trying hard to control himself, and I just loved that. To see that lovely sarcastic smile on his face and his failed attempt at not smiling -- I used to do that. People at the office sometimes seemed to be watching us or understanding something, but actually they were not ... and even if they were, who cared? For me now the office became the place where I was spending most of my lovely time. I became more serious in my job because of my extra caution thinking that he was my manager and may feel that I was living in my love shell and not working properly. I didn't want him to get this feeling in his mind. So I was working diligently and harder than ever before.

The days seemed to be shorter than I needed to express the way I was missing his hugs and his closeness even though he was in front of me whole day. I wanted to touch him, hug him, hide myself in his chest, dying for his scent which made me mad. But it was really hard to find a secure place where we two could be one for few moments. After lot of brainstorming, finally he came up with the idea that we could meet for few minutes in his house that was under construction, after the workers left for the day, and after we also left the office for the day. His under construction house wasn't a very romantic place, with dust on the floor, wet paint on the walls, wood and boards piled in every corner, nails all around, bare windows, and no curtains -- but who cared when we had no choice, and the desperation was mounted high?

I never felt that desperation, madness, and passion in him. He behaved very rationally and was always seemed to be in control of his emotions. That's what left me always in doubt regarding his love for me, or maybe I wanted to believe in the world I created on my own, which was full of his love, his thoughts, and him only. Regardless of my feelings, he always appeared to be normal. Sometimes I believed that our professional relationship was holding him back from showing how much he loved or cared for me deep inside his heart. He was trying hard not to be unfair with his position related to our professions, which could be later on manipulated by anybody for any personal benefit. I felt that he always had that fear at the back of his mind due to his hard-earned position and wealth, while I was all aloof and never acknowledged what he might be going through as a man. I was empathetic to him for what he explained, but his unspoken words never reached me. I was immature and too lost in his love to understand all that. It was a conjunction of different personalities altogether, he being the director, rule follower, authoritative type; while I am creative, adventurous, passionate, and love to go by my own rules, no matter even if they are against the world. In order to understand him more, I needed more time with him alone, which we were not getting. It was me always asking him for his time; it was me who wanted to meet him. He never showed any desire from his side for any secluded meeting. Often that initiated a thought storm in my mind that he was trying to stay away from me, as I was getting emotionally involved, while his sole intention was to enjoy me and have fun. After a lot of persuasion, he used to agree to those meetings, which at times were surprising. All this was a signal to me to start looking into his contradictions, which I could not understand, and being a secret matter I could not even discuss it with anybody to get a second opinion about my doubts.

Our love and romance continued in that house, though

we met only a few times. We managed to make excuses to our life partners for being late from the office. I was getting attached to him more than I was before. Obsession inside me was growing day by day, unaware of his intentions.

He had his birthday that day and he already warned me not to purchase any gift for him, as he wouldn't be able to justify that to his wife. My mind took his warning seriously and I didn't buy a gift for him. But my heart didn't understand that and I finally ordered a bouquet of beautiful dark-red roses, which were delivered to him. The roses were on his desk, and after few hours he called a meeting in his office. When everybody asked him who had given him those beautiful red roses, one of the ultimate creations of God, he wasn't able to explain it, and started talking about the matter for which he called everybody into his office, and in between he acknowledged through his eyes the receipt of those flowers from me, and I smiled and kissed him secretly -- he suddenly stammered and stopped speaking and laughter burst inside my heart, something we explained to each other through our eyes. We became expert at communicating through our eyes, as there were many things we could not speak aloud. Another way we communicated was through emails; we used to play email-email using our personal email ids without realizing that it was like storing the nuclear power for future blasts. He used to write few words and shorter emails, but those few words always touched me and I don't remember how many times I used to read them, and I still do that.

While going through all the romantic encounters, we

had fears deep down in our hearts that something someday might be a problem for both of us -- what if our secret love was revealed to our life partners? But we kept moving, without thinking too much about it, just ensuring our safety from day to day. We used to talk freely while we were driving back home; my home was near the office, so I used to stay in my parking area to talk to him a little longer, until he reached home. Weekends were too long to pass time without talking, without seeing each other, just waiting eagerly to meet on Monday. Every Monday morning when I saw him, it felt like I was breathless, dying to hug him and kiss him once -- the small distance was creating more closeness which was ought to last forever.

After a few days my marriage anniversary happened; right from the first Anniversary, my husband never celebrated or counted that day in our lives, and considered it the most useless day of his life --he wished he could have deleted it, from the calendar and his life. He had this belief due to the fact that after the marriage his career was suffering. Although his career failure had many reasons, rather than just astrological and superstitious reasons, everybody just seemed to close their eyes, as it is too easy make anything superstitious rather than actively investing energy to find out the alternatives and solutions. While it wasn't the same with me, as I always learned to be positive and hopeful about life, and my parents took all the pains to get me married, so I always considered that day to be their dream day. Since my relationship with my husband was not of an emotional type, I knew this time he would also disregard our 8th Anniversary and would stay in his own cocoon, waiting to become a butterfly sometime. I decided to change the meaning of this day in my life, and let my love be my life partner from this day onward. If you believe, then stone statues are equal to God, and all the unknown bonds exist, otherwise even the living humans don't matter. Somehow I started believing that my Love was my life partner -- I was treating him mentally as my husband, and my life shared with my real husband felt like I was cheating on my love. While it should be vice versa, I should be guilty for cheating on my husband, but it wasn't like that; it was opposite of that. All my respect, love, and regard for my husband were now transferred to my Love. The reason I am saying transferred is because this was not the case in the beginning with my husband when I got married to him. But life started taking a bad turn exactly after six months of our marriage, and slowly only pain and despair were left inside my heart. I respected and loved my parents too much, and in India an arranged marriage is considered more of a social event; divorce was not something on my mind due to the painful feeling that my parents might experience, or the agony that my child might go through.

Due to the feelings of true love and respect, I decided to spend my marriage anniversary day with my love. Luckily his wife was leaving the town for two days at the same time. So we had the space and peace to be together for the whole day. I came to office in Saree (Indian Traditional Dress) that day and then after two or three hours we left for his house.

We hugged each other, kept chatting and chirping around, and then he undressed me, so lovingly, and we made love. I felt like I was going through the "First Night" tradition of an Indian marriage with him. That day, my standards for him reached another height. I started looking at him as my life partner, as my husband, whatever you want to say -- somebody with whom I would share the rest of my life, somebody who was part of my body and soul, and was also my responsibility as a life partner. He was the complete man for me, the one I always dreamt of. After coming home late that day, I prayed to God, that – Hey God, please let both of us remain together for the rest of our lives, and as of today, I consider him to be and trust in him as my Life Partner. The speed at which my love was climbing high … I don't know whether it was the same for him or not. I never got enough time to share all this with him and to understand how things were moving for him. Initially in a relationship, trust building is the most sensitive thing to happen, and both of us were trying our best not to give any negative feelings to each other, but I felt that for him things were not changing the way they were for me.

Considering him as my life partner and trusting him deep down my heart brought another twist in my life. He was the father of two boys and always wanted a baby girl, a daughter whom he could love the most in his life. He told me this a few times, and I always remembered his thoughts about this matter. I started thinking along these lines -- I wanted to bear his child, wanted to deliver a baby girl of ours. The one who will be the living proof of our love and some part of him in her, would always be close to me, to fill the emptiness that I often used to feel while away from him. I kept thinking for few days about all this and tried to do the basic research work on my end, and then finally discussed it with him. He was surprised to hear my thoughts, and rejected the idea. I had long discussion sessions with him to make him understand why I wanted to do that, and how we could do it. But he was not getting a fair idea of what it might involve -- For him it was risky, scary, and something which could have negative permanent repercussions in his life. I tried to explain him that I would not let him suffer in any way, because I love him too much. But it seemed he was ignorant of what he meant to me and how I had started looking at our relationship. I did not understand whether his reluctance in this matter spoke of mistrust of himself, or of me. I understood that it was a complicated and sensitive matter, but when we were so much into the relationship and since I was dedicated to him, what was he really afraid of? Sometimes his extra cautious behavior and too fearful mentality seemed unjustified to me, considering that he was a man and I was the woman. A person needs to be courageous enough to take steps for future; to give direction to a relationship and to sustain it, and courage only comes from the strong bonds of love. The stronger the bond, the deeper the love inside, the more you will have the guts to take it forward. But he never had guts, and the reason was that he never had that level of love inside his heart for me. It was more like an infatuation for him, where he himself might be confused in trying to justify his physical involvement with me.

His major concern was what if tomorrow our life partners came to know about our affair. My justification for this was that they needed to understand us. We lived and were living our lives with them; we were committed to them to some extent now and to the fullest in our past, always committed financially and somewhat mentally now too -- we were good parents for our kids with them, and so we were indulging this love in our life now ,and if they can live with that, then it was good -- otherwise, everybody had the choice to walk away. I believe that marriages might be made in heaven, but are sustained by both the life partners. His wife and my husband -- both were lacking interest in us, and so whatever happened was justified at that time. Everybody has the option to leave anytime, if they feel suffocated and do not want to continue. Even after being suffocated and dealing with disinterested life partners, he and I both continued our marriages for years for the sake of our kids, sacrificing our satisfaction, as it was easy to find new partners for ourselves, but it was a challenging task to find equally good parents for our kids. That was one of the major reasons behind it. Although if we would have decided, even this notion might have been proved wrong, as I could be a loving mother for his kids too, and he would have been an equally good father for mine. If we hadn't been in India, and bound by Indian cultural ideas, then separation would have been the first option chosen by all of us. Thinking all this, I was determined to give birth to our own baby, but he was not feeling confident about it. He was indecisive, though the whole responsibility was mine.

I was not ready to let this drop, and slowly I was trying to make him understand and believe in the future which held our daughter. The most important point was that his belief in the future was missing, and he was always worried about his married life. It was the opposite for me; my belief in our future was certain, and the fear for my married life was none, as I was already living on the verge of ending it and it was merely a social relationship for me and nothing more. His fears for his married life were at times quite annoying for me, as if it was that important to him, then why was he still growing and sustaining the relationship with me? And if he wanted to maintain and live both lives, then he had certain responsibilities toward me too; some part of his life belonged to me too, otherwise it was nothing more than sexual interest. All these thoughts were torturous for my soul. If I considered that he was in love with me, but had limitations due to his married and social life, we were mature enough to find out ways, if we wanted to sustain it. He should have believed in the future of our love, like me. But he did not believe in it, and that used to give me pain at that time, and still does today. I am still living that future, not with him, but still for him. Living in the past is a waste of time, after the lesson is learned, but living in future gives your mind enough power and opens all the windows to receive solutions from eternity. That power can wake up the sleeping volcano inside hearts, and things can be revived to last forever only if I continued to believe in it.

While he was into the process of understanding all this, the time came for disaster to strike. Late at night, I was accessing my personal emails and suddenly there was a power outage, and after few minutes my laptop just turned off. I went to bed, and then as it was Saturday next day, I woke up a little late in the morning, only to find out that my husband had read all those hundreds of emails shared between me and my love -- my husband and I used to share the same laptop. He was able to access my emails because of the restored session when the power came back on, and he was awake quite early in the morning. I wasn't expecting this to happen so early … I knew it would happen, but this wasn't the right time. C'mon, we never are prepared for such events, and there is never the right, wrong ,or enough time for all this.

The moment I woke up, my husband said he had read all my emails and what was going on? Well, I was speechless for few minutes; I was trying to figure out what to say and how to start, as all my beginnings and endings were already revealed to him through those emails. So actually I had nothing to say or change or confess. I accepted that "Yes" this is what it is and I love him -- as you have read the emails, you might have gotten an idea of why all this started in my life and why and how I distanced myself from the marriage. I was trying to explain him the reason behind all that and I asked, what next? What do you want to do? He was silent, trying to control his anger. He told me that he needed time to think about it, and then he would discuss it with me.

Even though he said that, he started the discussion with me regarding the justification for the affair, and a fight raged between us which was the beginning of a war. During that day, I kept struggling alone on the battlefield, as it was the weekend, so I could not call my love to let him know what had happened. I tried to cool down my husband by telling him that I would stop and would limit myself, though he knew I could not leave my job immediately, being the main wage earner of the family. That seemed to me the only way to calm him down for a while, to get to a point when I could discuss it rationally with him.

Even after lots of assurance from my side, he wasn't in a frame of mind to trust what I was saying -- and how could he? The way he was living his life with me, he always felt in control of everything, taking me for granted for eight long years, and imposing his decisions on me most of the time. He never settled down mentally for all those decisions which I took after following him for seven years, which were not in line with his ideologies, and he always kept grudges against me in his heart , in a long list of negatives about me.

When Monday came, I went to the office and discussed with my love what had happened, and he was shocked. I never understood what was going on in his mind and how he was taking it, but one thing was sure -- he was unhappy and restless. Being a man, he might have his own fears and his own strategy to deal with such issues.

My home become like hell. Every day there were fights; yelling and blaming by my husband sucked the life out of me. The more I tried to explain to him, the more it went south. His suspicion seemed neverending. He blamed me for everything bad in his life, and made me the cause of all his failures, which he had already been in the habit of doing now and then. Every day, my love used to ask me how things were and at times, I only had tears in my eyes without any words. He used to give me some suggestions from time to time, about how I could handle things here and there. I was afraid like a child about what I was going through and wanted my love to step in, but I didn't know whether it was the right thing to do or not. I was finding it very hard to explain to my love what I was going through. I was spending lots of sleepless nights; I lost the mental balance to work in the office normally and had nobody to even talk to or discuss about what was happening, and matters were getting worse day by day.

Two months passed like this, when I decided I couldn't take it anymore -- earlier it was only suffocating but I got the option to go out and breathe for a while, but now it was choking; I could not live like this and I needed my life back, no matter the cost. So I asked for a divorce from my husband. When I said that, he was silent and told me he needed some time. I said OK, think about it, but we cannot continue like this -- it's better to go our own route and live happily. After two or three days he started to calm down and come to a point of agreement where he thought we should give our relationship another try. I agreed. My responses to my love were limited now, as I wasn't emailing him and we were talking for few minutes only and I was returning home on time from the office even though at times I had work to do. My husband was keeping an eye on me; I don't know in how many ways. Things started moving, but still every now and then he was scratching his own and my wounds. One thing that he understood was that love was missing from my life, and so all this happened. So he started showing me that he cared and he loved me. It wasn't that easy to change the life which I had been living with him during the last eight years. My husband wanted to go and meet my love in the office – I told him, if you do anything bad to him in public or in private, that will be the last day, the last moment that I will live in this house with you. That will be your last step and after that, I might die but will never come back in your life. I stopped him, because I knew that he was an angry man and might not be able to manage his anger on the spot.

Two more months passed like this, dealing with this mess at home every now and then, but finally things cooled down for the better after four months, and I took a deep breath. But this wasn't what God had planned for me and my love. Though we were not involved physically, love cannot be switched off just like that. So we were still talking to each other and were messaging each other over our cell phones. I was making sure that I was deleting every message immediately after reading it or writing it. But I don't know why he was not doing the same religiously. Maybe he was confident in the situation at his house, and feeling he was in full control of his married life. And when you are over-confident, you make mistakes. He and I shared some lovely messages that evening and the next morning, his wife just casually picked up his phone and read all that. Now whatever I had gone through in the past four months started for him. After a few calls here and there, his wife was able to find out that I was somebody who worked in the same office, because she had a close friend who also worked in the same office on the same floor, and used to sit nearby to my cubicle.

I received a call from his wife -- she was crying furiously and was scolding me left and right for what I was doing, and her sole intention was to make me understand that it was only me who is after her husband and her husband is naïf enough and not emotionally involved. That time I did not understand that she is a "Manipulative Mary" and that she had started that by all her means. I never manipulated anybody in my life, and I didn't knew how to handle this kind of difficult personality. She might be right in her position as a wife who dedicated her life solely to her husband and her kids, and always stood by him. The sound of her fear of loss and insecurity was loud enough to burst in my heart. She wanted her husband back, by any means; she wanted that control of love and power back, which I snatched from her. But she never understood that true power of control comes when you let somebody go and he or she decides not to go and chooses to stay with you forever, rather than consciously controlling and trying to possess a person by checking his emails and call logs and keeping track of all this. The one who stays in control in your life after all this effort is actually not meant for you. Leave him; if he comes back, he is yours. I could not explain all this to her, due to her life threatening ways of managing the issue. She was going through an emotional trauma, a sense of being cheated and feeling worthless. She could have run her life in a different way, if she only knew that taking people for granted doesn't work in the long run, and how important it is to keep married life lively in every sense.

She called me up again and again, and she wanted to know everything -- whatever happened between us, I still don't know why she wanted to know how many times we made love and even how we did it. Her questions were very offensive and I was, at times, scared of her crying. I was trying hard to conceal every personal fact from her and was not giving her any direct straight answers. Her anger and emotional outbursts were out of my control. I reached the office and talked to my love, and I told him what was happening, he kept listening silently, as he himself was dealing with her female tantrums and was being threatened by her in every way. She was threatening him trying to preserve her life. He was under emotional attack badly which was visible in his face and his actions. I tried to ask him if I could be of any help, but he refused and said he would manage by himself.

These kinds of issues between an Indian husband and wife often reach to the parents, which creates even more emotional pressure. This all was going on, and then I came to know that the lady friend of his wife in our office had started playing the role of a spy. Other than contacting me to find out everything, and involving my love's parents to pressure him, now she had involved her friend too. This became the real problem, because that was hampering even my normal work.

To this day, I wonder why all these people were trying to take control of our lives. Where were these people when we were facing difficulties in our marriage but still continuing it by fixing issues here and there, and how come it was their business now? My love's wife was checking his call logs and his email at every moment. He was not able to work properly in the office, and both of us were suffering under the manipulative control of his spouse. She was calling me to find out every detail and I was surprised by her courage, as her questions were too personal to answer. When she felt that I was not giving her the details she wanted, she took another deadly step.

I came home very tense due to all this, and my husband asked me right away, so you didn't stop all this? I asked why was he saying so? He said my love's wife called him and told him everything. Oh no, not again -- I was clueless and just didn't feel like saying a word. But my husband was totally in the mood to start all that again and was interested in finding out to what degree our affair was still going on. I had no choice but to listen to him and answer accordingly. I explained him that it was nothing more than the few messages that we shared, and things cannot be stopped suddenly, and I was trying to overcome all this. But all that went on all night. I tried to convince him that he should not talk to my love's wife and should not give any details to her. He didn't say a word. Maybe he also got a way to wage that power war against me; now he felt he could be in control of the situation as much as he thought he should be. Now the mess was everywhere for both of us, at home and in the office, and we were badly trapped.

Involving my husband in all this was a pathetic move by his wife. Because when my husband and I were going through all this during the last four months, we never involved her or anybody who was in contact with my love. This showed how much understanding my love and his wife had in their married life. This also proved that my love was badly in total control of his wife all his life through and that was the reason he was never able to reveal his true feelings to me. The law of marriage protects the rights of women, and at times they take negative advantage of that. And for a man it becomes a matter of shame in the society that he lives in, if he is either discarded by his wife or if he lives at home controlled by his wife.

While dealing with all this, suddenly I felt that my love had started behaving strangely to me. I wanted to talk to him to straighten all this out, and to map out a strategy to deal with it, so that I could understand what his wife was up to, and explain to him what my husband was doing. But he was not available to me at all. He was not able to talk in the office, not even over the phone. Also he was trying not to meet somewhere outside. I was unable to understand what he was trying to do, and what he was trying to accomplish. I knew he accepted responsibility in front of his wife, that he was equally involved. My mind was full of confusion, trying to figure out what I should do. How should I convey to him what I wanted? He was full of fear beyond my imagination. This lack of communication between us started taking a toll on our relationship. But I tried not to react to this, as I believed this would pass too. I was cooperating as much as I could.

We were paralyzed by the situations all around us. Both of us needed a time out, but how and where? Finally his wife and my husband were in touch with each other; maybe they planned a strategy against us in such a way that they made me look bad in front of my love, and my husband started convincing me about what all this is for a man, and how he dealt with the situation and with a woman like me. My husband sketched a very bad picture of my love in front of me by including our corporate relationship in between. I knew all this wasn't true, but things were not in my control -- I was trying hard to get some private time to talk to my love, which was being made impossible by the Spy friend of his wife, as she was keeping track of how much he was in the office, and whether he was going out or not. I was not aware that his wife has such a close friend in our office -- I knew they were friends, but I had no clue that it could be at this level. I was being interrogated and pressured all the time by my husband and my love's wife, and was also feeling pressured in the office due to that spy. Already I had suffered at home during the last four months and was left with no mental energy to go through all this anymore. For me it was becoming a case of "do or die." I was losing my energy to fight, and this loss of energy was largely due to the lack of communication between me and my love, because I was not able to think what should be done. I could not change the whole situation by myself -- I needed his support badly, but it was missing altogether.

Our company used to arrange a huge party for one of the most famous religious festivals of India, called Diwali. We all had plans and things to do for that special eve, as it's like Christmas for us Indians. I had plans with my team to be there with my family, when my love asked me not to come to that party as he would be there with his wife. This was awkward. I just couldn't process it. Was he trying to keep me out of every nook and cranny of this world, wherever his wife might go? Was his wife up to creating a scene in public? Was this the way to keep me away -- that he started controlling even this aspect of my life, where I should go and where I should not? This was not acceptable to me. I was also working for the same company, and it should not be under his control and authority. We were all adults dealing with something which could be sorted out by talking face to face. Instead he was trying to sort out the issue by covering it from here and there. I was angry and went to the party, despite his request that I should not attend. I was feeling rejected and isolated; the same might have been true of feelings inside his wife's heart, as she was a woman too. This evening made me feel that I was a small and powerless entity in comparison to my love, and whatever was going on between us was really a socially shameful act, as he looked very self-contained, and was surrounded by his family. The next morning at the office, my love was annoyed by my presence in that party. He was trying to stop me, as he didn't want his wife to be in more pain than she was already going through. Suddenly his lost love for his wife bubbled up and he was too concerned about her, regardless of what I went through and was going through. Is the relationship on paper in the form of a Marriage Certificate and approved by society the only relationship that has meaning? Love is nothing? It's just a nice name given to the physical pleasures which cannot be achieved within the boundaries of married life? Was I being used by him only for his intimate desires? These thoughts were disgusting to me – and then another event happened to confirm these sickening thoughts. Our company sponsored a camping trip for two days with family as a bonus and recreational activity for our hard work. My love was the one who was organizing the whole show. This time he exercised his power and authority to stop me from going. No matter how much I begged him to include me, he just remained tight lipped and didn't include my name on the list to go. I did not say anything, and everybody left for the two-day camping trip. I was in office for those two days trying to figure out what was going on. Why was he doing all this to me? I was trying to analyze now up to what extent he would exercise his power and authority. It was now clear to me, after this event, that he was trying to find a way to make me quit my job.

At last one day, in the office, my love simply asked me –

Why don't you leave this job? It's easy for you, you can get another job, and things will be all right for all of us. I was stunned by his statement, as too many things were going on in my mind. I was under the influence of manipulation by my husband, by my love's wife, and most of all, by my love himself. But still I was trying to manage everything. It had been five months for me now, since I had started dealing with all this.

I listened to him quietly; I was not able to believe what he had just said. So he decided that he wanted to throw me out of his life now, when I had reached the point where I was ready to give up everything I had? I was broken by his statement – it was midnight, and I was still sitting in the office, crying in my chair. I was crying so badly, that another manager came to my desk and asked what had happened? I controlled myself not to say a word and he kept asking and asking again. I was broken that night -- something which I had held onto and had fought for during the past five months was now going out of my life. After that manager insisted, as he was a good friend of mine, I instantly invented a story about a professional misunderstanding, and explained something to him which was different from the truth. Then he tried to console me and finally came with me to drop me at home, as I was not even in a safe condition to drive -- I left my car in the office parking lot. My heart was churning with thoughts; I hated the level of his power which my love was now using for his personal benefit. I had a nervous breakdown at home that night; my blood pressure reached a dangerous low point, and I felt like my heart had just stopped beating. My husband was awake and waiting for me at home, and he understood from my face that something was seriously wrong with me; I only told him that I was not feeling well -- it seemed like my blood pressure is too low and while I was telling him all this, I fainted. I don't know what happened then – I woke up in the morning and my father, being a doctor, was sitting next to me -- he asked me what had happened and how it happened? I was silent as a stone. It was the weekend, so I was at home; my body was lying and resting on the bed for the next two days, but my mind was still in a hurricane. Finally I reached the conclusion that if his wife was so good and if my love only wanted her in his life, and if I was just nothing to him, then I should really look for a new job and leave as soon as possible. I understood that I was giving his wife enormous pain, for no reason. When I reached the office on Monday, I was much more stable and was behaving with unnatural calm, with suppressed feelings in my heart, just working like a machine on whatever was required. I applied for every possible opening and during the next week I had two offers in my hands. I planned to accept one of them; it was not very far away from my current office. I was so angry at my love and at all that was going on -- I didn't even wish to serve the required notice period. I went inside my love's office to tell him that I was resigning today and the day after tomorrow, Friday, would be my last working day there. He said, "What?" And he asked why I was leaving. To this day, I do not understand why he questioned me, because he was the one who asked me to leave. Anyway, my answer to him was "Are you asking me why? Is there any reason left to stay?" I said that from a different perspective and I don't know what he understood from all that. But he accepted my resignation and I left. I joined another company. Things were still not settled in my heart, I was broke, I was devastated from every angle -- I still wanted him back in my life even though he handled everything for his own personal benefit. I was ready to bear any cost. I wrote him letters, which risked being intercepted by his wife. I was too distracted and disturbed to do good work at the new company, as most of the time I was only thinking about bringing him back to my life -- he meant everything to me, I belonged to him and he just left me alone; he was my life and the reason to live. But all my attempts to bring him back were in vain … he only gave me an understanding that I should leave and go away from his life.

My hours were spent outside my new office to call him, to talk to him, but he always seemed to be busy and had no time for me. His behavior was life-threatening to me. After trying and trying in every way to bring him back during the next month and a half, another company approached me for an immediate US assignment. But they wanted me to relocate to a different city, far away from my current place of employment. I did not accept the offer to relocate my family, and just went alone to that other city and took the job. I was still not out of all that had happened in my life. And one day while talking to my love's wife, and when she cried again, and begged me to leave her husband alone, I assured her that I would go as far away from their life as possible and would not create any reason to bother them again in any way.

And finally I left India and came to the US alone. Living alone without my little kid was very hard for me, considering that I had already gone through more than six months of emotional turbulence for a love affair of six months. I tried to email him once or twice, and every time the email was read by his wife and she responded to me. I was not being informed by my love that I should not email him on his usual email IDs, as his wife was reading everything, and this was the problem since the beginning. In the starting also I come to know by her wife, that she was reading my emails, not by him and that was really bad to me. Anyway, I stopped writing email to him and stopped calling him, thinking that he had gone from my life and he wanted it to be that way.

Now due to the way it ended, I had a belief in my heart, that he never loved me -- he just used me for his physical pleasure. If this was my perception, then this is what he let me believe. He never called me to explain anything to me, to explain his side of the story, his pains that he went through -- so I never got an idea of what it was for him, and why he disconnected all the channels of communication between me and him. He knew my phone number always; he had the time and opportunity to talk to me anytime. He had my email IDs to provide me an explanation. Wasn't it his responsibility to do that for a person like me, who was treating him like her life partner? The one who was ready to bear his child -- wasn't all that enough to show him how much I loved him, and how much I cared? Did I have to die to show him what he meant to me? I wasn't playing with him, but I got the feeling that he was playing with me.

This traumatic event of my life almost killed me from within. For a long time I was just unable to sleep at night. I had no idea how to fix myself. I still find it hard to forget my love, though my life is keeping me busy enough. Deep in my mind I always keep analyzing what happened between me and my love and why it ended the way it ended -- my agonies were endless and my world just seemed to be upside down all the time. I never questioned his desire to keep his marriage alive, but the way he did it was wrong. Even though it ended badly, I just couldn't stop loving him. I loved him; I still love and will always love him.

I still talk to him mentally and spend time with him alone in my heart. I cannot change my belief that converted into the conviction that I belong to him, and one day on this earth while living and before I die, I will be with him again. He loved me -- my heart always says that to me, though my conscious always challenges that belief.

It's been four years of a roller coaster ride of feelings of pain and feelings of despair. Wasn't all that disgusting enough to teach me a lesson? Or is this something that I want to explain to the whole world, since I feel I was unable to explain it to him?

The stage where I am right now gives me a better understanding of what happened and how things were laid out. Four years back it all started with something called Infatuation, and then from my side only it changed into Love, and as time passed it became serene and divine love, a love that could withstand anything on this earth, a love that was at times humiliating too due to the reactions of our spouses.

It's been four years now and still I feel empty. It feels like nothing is left inside, it's just pain and tears. I didn't forget anything -- every minute of every day I spent with and without him is still in my eyes and I live with it day and night, months and years.

Isn't that punishment long enough for loving somebody and seeing him for six months? Sometimes I just think -- how can I still love him silently? But then I feel if I love him, that's none of his business anymore. He is no longer the person whom I loved and is no longer man enough to face the world for what he did. He cannot even stand my silent love. At times I wonder whether I love him or I hate him. Hatred, when it reaches its height of intensity, becomes like love, and never leaves your heart alone. Love and hatred both gives you the same burning deep inside your heart.

He lives with his last perception that "something very ugly happened between us" and I live with "something very lovely happened between us."

A saga of love will continue till the end of eternity……..

About the Author

Zsofia has written articles in leading newspaper and magazines like "IT" and "Developer IQ." She also appeared on talk shows on All India Radio for two years. She has successfully covered the technical documentation for hundreds of software requirements and has prepared excellent material for help guides. She blogs and advises people in need. Her short stories and poetry were always in the school and college year magazines. She has the fire inside to represent the burning social and behavioral issues of the society with a different perspective. She is excited about her book and welcomes suggestions and critiques at zsofia70@yahoo.com. Her blog - http://zsofiaterrene.blogspot.com/ has some very useful suggestions regarding relationships, as she believes "Prevention is better than a cure.." Divorce Attorneys and Psychologists are there when you need a fix, but prevention costs less, so why not start right at this moment? Alerting others of danger is another way of reducing the depression in relationships and society. Voicing together with her in saving other women is never too late.

LaVergne, TN USA
02 November 2009
162752LV00001B/77/P